FOX IN LOVE

FOX IN LOVE

by Edward Marshall
pictures by James Marshall

DIAL BOOKS FOR YOUNG READERS
NEW YORK

Dial easy-to-read

For Benedict Clouette

Published by
Dial Books for Young Readers
A Division of NAL Penguin Inc.
2 Park Avenue
New York, New York 10016
Published simultaneously in Canada by
Fitzhenry & Whiteside Limited, Toronto

Printed in Hong Kong
COBE
4 6 8 10 9 7 5

The Dial Easy-to-Read logo is a registered trademark of
Dial Books for Young Readers, a division of NAL Penguin Inc.,
® TM 1,162,718.

Library of Congress Cataloging in Publication Data
Marshall, Edward. Fox in love.
Summary: Fox falls in love with several girls
and then enters a dance contest with his sister.
[1. Foxes—Fiction.]
1. Marshall, James, 1942– , ill. II. Title.
PZ7.M35655Fp   [E]   82-70190   AACR2
ISBN 0-8037-2426-8
ISBN 0-8037-2433-0 (lib. bdg)

The art for each picture consists of a black ink
line-drawing with three overlays reproduced
in red and green halftone and black tint.

Reading Level 1.8

FOX
IN LUCK

"Fox, dear," said Fox's mom.

"What did I do?" said Fox.

"I want you to take Louise

to the park," said Mom.

"I'm too busy," said Fox.

"You'll take Louise," said Mom.

"And that is that."

"No!" said Fox.

Mom gave Fox one of her looks.

"Oh, all right," said Fox.

"Of all the luck.

Come on, Louise."

"Tra-la-la-la," said Louise.

At the park

Louise had quite a bit of fun.

She played in the sandbox.

She hung upside down.

She played on the slide.

And she played on the swings.

"This is dumb," said Fox.

"Let's go home and watch TV."

Just then they saw

a pretty white fox.

She was all alone.

And she was having a fine time.

"Wow!" said Fox.

"She looks just like a movie star!"

"Hi!" said the pretty white fox.

"My name is Raisin."

All of a sudden Fox could not speak.

He forgot his own name.

"Hi!" said Louise.

"I'm Louise.

And this is my brother Fox."

Fox and Louise got on
the merry-go-round.

"You are sweet to bring
your little sister to the park,"
said Raisin.
"I love to do it," said Fox.
Louise gave Fox a look.

"This is more fun than TV,"
said Raisin.

"Oh, yes," said Fox.

"I never watch TV."

Louise gave Fox another look.

"Oh, dear," said Raisin.

"I am late for my piano lesson."

"I love the piano," said Fox.

"See you again," said Raisin.

And she left the park.

"Wow!" said Fox.

17

The next day

Fox found Louise in her room.

"Time for the park," he said.

"I'm too busy," said Louise.

"You can bring your dolly," said Fox.

"She doesn't like the park,"
said Louise.

"You are going to the park," said Fox.

"And that is *that*!"

"You can't make me!" said Louise.

"I will buy you a hot dog,"

said Fox. "With onions."

"Let's go," said Louise.

And off they went.

At the park, Fox spent his last dime.

"There's Raisin," said Louise.

"Hello," said Raisin. "I *love* hot dogs!"

"Oh, dear," said Fox.

"I just spent my last dime."

And he gave Louise such a look!

"Then I will buy you a hot dog,"
said Raisin.
"I am very rich."

"Wow!" said Fox.
"This is my lucky day!"

FOX AND THE GIRLS

On Monday

Fox and Millie went to the fair.

"Let's have our picture taken,"

said Fox.

"Oh, yes, let's do," said Millie.

24

"Click" went the camera.

And out came the pictures.

"Sweet," said Millie.

"One for you and one for me,"
said Fox.

On Tuesday

Fox and Rose went to the fair.

"How about some pictures?"

said Fox.

"Tee-hee," said Rose.

"Click" went the camera.

And out came the pictures.

"Tee-hee," said Rose.

"I'll keep mine always,"

said Fox.

On Wednesday

Fox and Lola went to the fair.

"I don't have a picture of us,"

said Fox.

"Follow me," said Lola.

"Click" went the camera.

And out came the pictures.

"What fun!" said Lola.

"I'll carry mine everywhere."

"Me too," said Fox.

On Thursday

Fox and Raisin went to the fair.

"Ooh! I want a picture," said Raisin.

"Fine idea," said Fox.

"Click" went the camera.

And out came the pictures.

"Don't we look silly,"

said Raisin.

"A scream," said Fox.

The next day Fox was
showing off for Raisin.

And some pictures
fell out of his pocket.
Raisin picked them up.

"Well!" she cried.

"Wait until the girls

hear about this!"

And on Saturday

Fox went to the fair ...

all alone.

"Click."

FOX
TROT

Fox was a fine dancer.

He could waltz.

He could boogie.

He could do the stomp.

"That Fox really *moves*!" said Dexter.

One day Fox decided to enter
THE BIG DANCE CONTEST.
"Who will be my partner?" he asked.
"Don't look at me," said Carmen.
"I don't dance."

"Why not ask Raisin?" said Dexter.

"She's a great dancer."

"She's mad about something," said Fox.

"Ask her anyway," said Carmen.

"Here she comes now."

"Uh," said Fox.

"Yes, what is it?" said Raisin.

"Will you be my partner in

THE BIG DANCE CONTEST?" asked Fox.

"Are you sure you are good enough?"
said Raisin.

"Don't worry about *that*!" said Fox.

Every day Fox and Raisin

practiced hard for

THE BIG DANCE CONTEST.

They did the waltz.

They did the boogie.

They did the stomp.

They even did the Fox trot.

Raisin was very good.

But she was still mad about something.

"I'm sure they will win

first prize," said Dexter.

On the day of

THE BIG DANCE CONTEST

Fox went to Raisin's house.

"Sorry, Fox," said Raisin's mom.

"Raisin has the mumps."

"Oh, no!" cried Fox.

Fox went home.

He sat down

in front of the TV.

But he didn't even turn it on.

He was too upset.

Suddenly he had an idea.

"Come here, Louise!" he cried.

"What did I do?" said Louise.

"Just do what I say," said Fox.

"First put your right foot here.

And then put your left foot there."

Louise did as she was told.

Louise was a fast learner.
Soon they were dancing
around the room.
Fox looked at his watch.
"Let's go!" he cried.

THE BIG DANCE CONTEST was on.

"Fox and his partner are next,"
called out the judge.

Fox was nervous.

"Calm down," said Louise.

And the music began.

Fox and Louise did the waltz.

They did the boogie.

They did the stomp.

And the crowd went wild.

"How did you do?" said Dexter.

"We won second prize," said Fox.

"Next year we will win first!"
said Louise.

"You said it!" said Fox.

7139

E
MAR   Marshall, Edward.

Fox in love.

DANIEL ST. THOMAS JENIFER
ELEMENTARY SCHOOL

813586 54767D 05843F